MOVING MOLLY

SHIRLEY HUGHES

THE BODLEY HEAD

London

Other picture books by
SHIRLEY HUGHES

Alfie Gets in First
Alfie Gives a Hand
Alfie's Feet
An Evening at Alfie's
The Big Alfie and Annie Rose Storybook
Dogger
Helpers
Sally's Secret
Up and Up

For Clara

British Library Cataloguing
in Publication data
Hughes, Shirley
Moving Molly
I. Title
823'.9'IJ PZ7.H/
ISBN 0 370 30125 0
Copyright © Shirley Hughes 1978
Printed and bound in Great Britain for
The Bodley Head Children's Books
32 Bedford Square, London WC1B 3SG
by Cambus Litho, East Kilbride
Separations by Colourcraftsmen Ltd, Chelmsford
First published 1978
Reprinted 1982, 1984, 1988, 1989

Molly lived in the town.
There were one, two, three,
four, five, six, SEVEN
steps down to her front door
from the street.

When Molly was a little baby her Mum had to pull the
pram up the steps when they went out——bump,
bump, bump, bump, bump, bump,
BUMP!

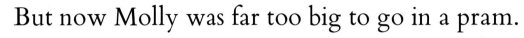

But now Molly was far too big to go in a pram.

Molly's big sister, Joanie, and her big brother, Patrick, played out on the pavement with the other children when they came home from school.

They had made Molly's old pram wheels into a go-cart, and they all whizzed up and down on it as far as the corner and back. Sometimes they gave Molly rides on it too.

From Molly's window you could see a lot of legs going by. Sometimes you could see cats, too, sitting on the railings. Mum said that she didn't much like seeing just legs and cats out of the window, but Molly liked them. She always watched out for her Dad's legs when it was time for him to come home from work.

Mum had some plants in pots on the window-sill to make the view look prettier. Molly often helped her water them. Some of the plants grew quite tall in the summer time, if the cats didn't come and scratch them up. Molly wished that they had a real garden, big enough to play in.

Then, one day, her wish came true!
Mum and Dad told the children that
they had found a house with a garden
for them all to live in! Right away
everyone began to make plans.

The very next Sunday Dad took them all to see the new house. It was quite a long way away. First they clattered round all the empty rooms, deciding where to put everything. Then they all went to look at the garden. It was long and thin, and it had a little lawn and some trees down at the bottom. Someone had left a lot of rubbish lying about in it. Molly thought that this looked quite interesting, but Dad said that there would be a lot of tidying up to do.

On moving day everything got piled up in funny places and there were boxes everywhere. A big van arrived with two men in it. They were called Gary and Les, and they could pick up furniture as though it wasn't heavy at all. They started to carry all the family things up the steps and into the van.

When they had finished the rooms looked very empty and strange. Even the carpets had gone from the floor. A piece of wall-paper was hanging loose off the wall where Molly's bed had been.

Molly lifted up the flap and wrote a very small 'M' for Molly underneath with a blue crayon. Then she stuck it down with spit because she knew she mustn't write on walls.

Then it was time to go. Gary and Les said that she could ride with them in the front of the big van if she was good. They helped her hop up beside them. It was very high up. The others all got into the little car behind. They were very low down. Then Gary started the engine.

They were off!

It was nearly dark when they arrived at the new house. The children ran up the path to their new front door. Gary and Les and Mum and Dad started to unload all the furniture, boxes and suitcases, and the empty rooms began to be full of jumbled-up things. When it was all done they had a cup of tea. Then Gary and Les said goodbye, and all the family went to wave them off in their empty van.

That evening Molly went off to bed in her little new bedroom. It was very exciting because she had never had a room of her very own before. She lay awake for a long time. It was very quiet outside with no footsteps passing by. But she could hear some cats calling to each other in the next door garden. Molly liked cats. She went off to sleep listening to them.

Now they all started to settle down in their new house. Every day Mum was busy painting and wall-papering and getting things in order. And every day, when Dad came home, he was busy in the garden.

Joanie and Patrick started their new school. They caught the School Bus every day at the end of the road. Sometimes Molly went to see them off. Molly wasn't big enough to go to that school, and she couldn't go to play-group either because it was too far away.

After school Patrick went about on his new two-wheeler, which he had just learnt to ride. And Joanie went to feed her new guinea-pig in his wooden house.

They were all very busy.

Molly hadn't very much to do.
There were no plants to water yet.

She looked over the gate,
but not many people seemed to be passing.
She climbed up and looked over the fence,
but the house next door was empty.

There was a field at the
bottom of the garden,
but there were no cows
in it, only grass.

She tried to talk to the
guinea-pig, but he was
fast asleep at the back of
his house and wouldn't
come out.

So Molly went to the rubbish heap to see if she could find anything interesting to play with. And there, behind the piles of old tins and bottles, she found a hole in the fence. It led to the garden next door. Molly slipped through the hole.

The grass on the
other side was very
long, higher than
Molly's head in
places, and it was all
grown up with weeds
and brambles.

It was a jungle for cats. Molly met a
black one walking through the grass,

and a ginger one and a striped
one washing themselves in
a patch of sunlight.

She found a green-house, leaning against a wall. It had no door, and some of its panes were broken. Inside were a lot of old plant pots. Molly looked at them. Some of them had plants growing in them.

When she went back for tea, Molly
didn't tell anyone about the hole
in the fence, or the over-grown garden
next door, or the green-house. But after this she went
there quite often. Sometimes she took some water in
an old jug, and gave the plants a drink.

There was always something to do in the next door garden. It was a good place to play in if you were by yourself.

One day Molly was swinging on the gate when she saw a big van coming up their road. At first she thought it was Gary and Les coming back, but it wasn't. They stopped at the house next door. Then they started to unload a lot of furniture and carry it inside.

Molly went upstairs to her little room and sat on her bed. All afternoon she heard people tramping up and down. Then she heard voices calling to each other in the next door garden. She knew that now it would belong to someone else, and that she wouldn't be able to slip through the hole in the fence any more. What would happen to the plants without her to give them a drink?

But next day Molly went down to the rubbish heap, and what do you think she saw? Two little faces, exactly alike, looking through the hole in the fence at her. They belonged to two little twins called Kathy and Kevin.

After this Molly found that there were a lot more things to do. She could play in the next-door garden, after all, with Kathy and Kevin. They helped her to water the plants in the green-house, because they liked doing that too. And she always got there by slipping through the hole in the fence. When Dad made a swing for her at last, Kathy and Kevin came through the fence to play in *her* garden. They all took turns on the swing, even though there was sometimes a lot of argument.

And when they found the old go-cart, made out of Molly's pram wheels, they took turns on that, too, whizzing up and down as far as the corner and back.

Wasn't it lucky it hadn't been thrown away in the move?

As for the cats——well, Kathy and Kevin's
Dad didn't get much time for gardening,
so they still had their jungle after all.